W9-CPZ-649

Dream Song

Walter de la Mare

Illustrated by

Monique Felix

Creative Editions

Sunlight, moonlight,
Twilight, starlight–

Gloaming at the close of day,

And an owl calling,
Cool dews falling
In a wood of oak and may.

Lantern-light, taper-light,
Torchlight, no-light:
Darkness at the shut of day,

And lions roaring,
Their wrath pouring
In wild waste places far away.

Elf-light, bat-light,
Touchwood-light and toad-light,

And the sea a shimmering gloom of grey,

And a small face smiling
In a dream's beguiling

In a world of wonders far away.

Designed by Rita Marshall

Published in 2019 by Creative Editions

P.O. Box 227, Mankato, MN 56002 USA

Creative Editions is an imprint of The Creative Company

www.thecreativecompany.us

Printed in China

Library of Congress Cataloging-in-Publication Data

Names: De la Mare, Walter, 1873–1956, author. / Felix, Monique, illustrator.

Title: Dream song / by Walter de la Mare; illustrated by Monique Felix.

Summary: This dreamy poem about all the kinds of light at the "shut of day" evokes a world of wonder.

Identifiers: LCCN 2018054976 / ISBN 978-1-56846-337-7

Subjects: LCSH: Light—Juvenile poetry. / Sun—Rising and setting—Juvenile poetry. / English poetry—20th century.

Classification: LCC PR6007.E3 D74 2019 DDC 821/.912—dc23

First edition 9 8 7 6 5 4 3 2 1